AEON OF CHAOS

It is the Aeon of Chaos, a time of terror, wonder, and pleasures undreamed of. The gods are dead and the great demons gnaw at their bones. From the cannibal kingdom of Kaszanka to the sordid pornocracy of Thune life is frenzied and cheap. Fortunes and kingdoms are bartered at the swing of a blade. Lawlessness and lust rule the day, while magic and mayhem take charge of the night. Slavery and massacre swarm across the land like ants at a picnic, while notes of demon laughter dance over all like shadows of flames from the deific pyre. It is the Aeon of Chaos, and only Chaos reigns!

The Court of the Mushroom King

Copyright © 2021 by B.J. Swann

Editing by Christine Morgan

Cover by Elizabeth Bedlam

Punk AF and Aeon of Chaos Logos designed by Caelan Stokkermans Arts

THE COURT OF THE MUSHROOM KING

BJ SWANN

Contents

CHAPTER 1: THE MUSHROOM PILGRIMS

It is the Aeon of Chaos. All the gods are dead, and the demons wear their entrails as lingerie.

Ziqqora arose well before dawn and snuck off across the manicured lawn bordering her father's crumbling castle. She didn't usually like to get up so early; she liked to sleep in and dream until the servants came to rouse her. Even then she'd often complain of a headache, or a stomach ache, or some other phantom malady, thereby lingering in bed until well after noon, slipping in and out of dreams until the fullness of the sun and the smell of cooking lunch finally called out to her. But this morning was different. She was off to do something forbidden, and did not want to be seen.

At length she came to the edge of the Royal Gardens, which was something of a misnomer, for this was not a place of orderliness, cut and curated, but a sprawl of unruly woodlands stretching on for miles, used primarily for hunting by the king and his cronies. Ziqqora knew the outskirts well, and often went walking in them, but today she was going much farther than usual.

And so she set off, passing thickets of oaks and crawling yews, stagnant pools filled with swarming little tadpoles, and rivulets bordered by reeds. She spied pheasants, ducks, and a solitary fox whose face was smeared with blood. He watched her warily, and with good reason, for many of his kin had been hunted to death by her father's black hounds, their bodies torn apart, their blood used to daub royal foreheads and season royal wine with a bitter iron tang.

Onward Ziqqora went. Steadily the woods became wilder. The canopy thickened, obscuring the slowly-rising sun. The servants in the palace would no doubt be up and about by now, preparing for the day. Ziqqora hoped the dummy she'd put in her bed, made from pillows and a wig, would fool them for a while – at least until she returned from her intended destination. But she didn't really know how far she had to go, nor even if she'd ever be back.

She felt a pulse of excitement as she strode through the darkening wood. She'd never gone this deep by herself before. The scenery turned into a shadowy haze of trees, leaves, and moist black earth. After a while her legs got tired and her body grew clammy with sweat. She stopped to eat a cake and some apples. Just how far was the bloody place anyway, she wondered? She'd been to the outskirts only once, long ago, in her earliest childhood, and could just barely remember a forbidding iron fence and the aura of mystery it seemed to contain.

She got up and kept walking, still wondering how much farther she had to go, until suddenly the old iron fence she was seeking hove up in the distance ahead, surrounded by shadows and trees.

At last! she thought, then stood there, staring.

The fence, like the castle she lived in, was twisted by age. The ground had shifted over time, turning the pickets askew. The gates were locked with chains so rusty and covered with lichen that the links had grown together. The forest beyond looked more or less like the one she'd just passed through – at least from the outside. The only hint of its special nature were the toadstools that grew along the edge and led off into its depths like a white-capped road.

The forbidden garden beyond the fence had been a mystery tormenting her for years. All she knew was it contained a lot of mushrooms. And what was the big deal about that? She ate mushrooms for dinner; everyone did. So why, then, should this garden be off-limits? No one would give her an answer. Not her father the king, certainly not her stepmother. Not the cooks, tutors, chamberlains, scullery maids, seamstresses, chimney sweeps, stable lads, nor any other members of the vast household staff that bustled round the mansion like a horde of human bees.

At last, in desperation, she asked the groundskeeper, whom she tended to avoid. It wasn't because she didn't like him personally, but because of his son. Bertrand, the dirty brat, was always leering at her through the windows. He'd even been flogged for it, though not at her behest. Thus, she'd waited until the groundskeeper was alone in the field before approaching him with her questions.

"The garden wasn't always forsaken,' he'd said, smoking his pipe, black dirt clinging in the creases of his fingers. "Once, it was considered this kingdom's greatest treasure, on account of the mushrooms that grew there."

"Yeah, mushrooms, I know," she'd said. "What's the big deal?"

"Oh, these mushrooms were special. Magickal. They gave marvellous visions to anyone who ate them. So, your ancestors made the garden private royal property. No one else was allowed to go in there, on pain of death. They built a wall, and had it guarded night and day by their deadliest, most trustworthy knights. Then, only after solemn ceremonies and much preparation would a chosen few eat of the mushrooms and experience the visions."

"What'd they see?"

"Such secrets weren't shared with common folk. One thing's for sure, though – the knowledge they gained was powerful indeed. They used it to conquer their foes and bring peace to the realm. Some called them the Mushroom Kings, and their old coat-of-arms had a toadstool with a crown on the top. But then something bad happened."

"What?"

"Well, King Boletus – that would be your great-great-great grandfather – was especially keen on the mushrooms. Ate of them liberally. For a time he was the wisest of kings, but then he began to...overindulge. He'd go off to the garden for days at a time with his courtiers, enjoying his visions. Eventually, they didn't came back. When searchers finally found them, the king… he'd been transformed.

"A horrible sight, they say it was. His feet rooted to the ground, his flesh fibrous and pale, his very sweat a mist of white spores. As if he'd become a mushroom himself. After that, his heir – your great-great grandfather – had the whole place sealed off. He locked the gates and threw away the key, lest the kingdom's entire noble line be tempted to a similar fate."

"But why did they change?" Ziqqora had asked.

The old groundskeeper had merely shrugged. "No one really knows. Some think the fungus is alive. Not as plants are, but as men are. That beneath those caps and stalks are souls just as bright as our own, perhaps even brighter. That by eating of their flesh, one is able to commune with their slumbering minds. They say maybe old Boletus just got too greedy, and was punished for his gluttony. The 'shrooms had had enough of being eaten, and decided to punish all who might feast on them in future."

A chill now ran down Ziqqora's spine as she remembered the groundskeeper's tale. Imagine being transformed into a mushroom! Even more compelling than her fear, though, was her desire to experience such wondrous visions for herself.

Dreaming was her passion, after all. Her main pastime and escape.

There just wasn't much else for her to do with her life. The staff treated her like some kind of poisonous flower: beautiful, but untouchable. Get too close, the king might have their heads. Not even the randiest of handsome stableboys would be suicidal enough to sneak off with her into a field. The only one who seemed incorrigible enough was Bertrand, and he was gross!

No, other than him, no servant of either sex would ever risk corrupting her bearing with their common speech, their slovenly postures, or their un-royal ways. Her dad would have them flogged if he found her using gutter slang or slouching at her desk. Even the groundskeeper's language had turned more high-falutin in her presence, as if he'd been auditioning for the role of royal storyteller. Even so, after telling her the tale of the garden, he'd hustled away, afraid to be seen with her.

It left her only a mere handful of people with whom she

was permitted to associate: her father, who was always busy; her stepmother, whom she hated; her stepsisters, who picked on her constantly; and her tutors, a pack of stodgy old eunuchs who wouldn't know fun if it came up and bit them on the dismal remains of their testes. She had nothing else to do but wait for some prearranged marriage to some prince she'd never met. Even that, in a way, was its own form of dreaming. Sometimes, even a nightmare.

So, she spent her time dreaming of other things. The night offered its own kind of dreams, of course, but so did the mornings and afternoons, when she'd lie on the lawn and look up at the clouds, and daydream.

But, these fabled, forbidden mushrooms! Surely the visions they'd offer would be something else entirely – something transcendental, as lurid as a thousandfold suns!

Having found the iron fence, she looked for a means to get over it, skirting the edge until she found an oak whose upper branches had grown very close to the top. She climbed up cautiously, the task made harder by her long, lacy dress. Being a princess, she didn't have much in the way of practical attire.

The boughs shuddered and creaked underneath her, threatening to snap. She stepped off quickly, placing her slender little feet between the rusted iron spikes that jutted up from the topmost bar. The fence swayed, metal groaning. She crouched to grasp the spikes and stop herself tumbling from her teetering perch. Another spike poked rudely at her groin. Had she crouched any lower, she would've impaled herself upon it. Now wouldn't *that* be a stupid way to lose her virginity!

She steadied herself, the scabrous rusted metal rough on her delicate skin, then tipped forward and took a plunge into the garden. Her dress snagged and tore on the spikes as she fell, but she landed in the undergrowth and rolled, with no more harm done than messing her hair and dirtying her hands.

Jumping to her feet, she brushed herself off, and sighed with relief. She'd done it! Now all she had to do was find the grove at the centre of the garden, where grew those miraculous mushrooms!

The paths, long neglected, were well overgrown. She followed the trail of white-capped mushrooms, which became more numerous, not to mention more colourful. Vivid little toadstools teemed on all sides, some pink and powder-blue, others crimson and canary-feather yellow. Some looked like teeth with drops of blood on the top.

Before long, she saw mushrooms everywhere, and not just along the path. They covered the trees like fibrous cloaks; they clung to the rocks and the logs in tiers of brown wafers. Some were fibrous and long, like reeds underwater; others were fulsome and fat, with thick stumps and caps enough to sit on. The air hung heavy with moisture and a cloying, sweaty smell, not unlike the inside of a codpiece. Spore clouds sparkled in what light shot down through the canopy, dancing like dust in some musty old attic. Most of the mushrooms were beautiful, but some looked decidedly sinister. A black, mould-like fungus grew on some of the trees, seeming to seethe angrily.

Ziqqora gave that stuff a wide-berth and continued on for what seemed like ages, searching for the grove. At last, she came to a generous clearing dotted with massive, rainbow-coloured toadstools. Between them were shapes that looked like ancient statues, perhaps placed here to decorate the garden, long ago. She drew closer, then froze.

They weren't statues at all, but the remains of people. Her great-great-great grandfather and his courtiers, presumably. Their once-colourful clothing had faded with time. Their bodies were fibrous and white. Their elongated fingers looked like slender fungal shoots. Their bare feet lay sunken in the soil. Their skin was striped with gills, oozing a viscous red liquid that made them look like they were bleeding from a multitude of tiny little cuts. But their faces were smiling.

One of them wore a crown. His expression was of sheer ecstasy. Was this her ancestor, Boletus, the last of the Mushroom Kings? He didn't look as though his transformation had been painful at all. Ziqqora walked among the figures, her skin prickling with wonder and dread. Beside each of them was one of the huge toadstools. Their caps were a riot of colours, as if a painter had gone mad with his palette and created some vibrant abstraction. The meat looked soft, tender. It scintillated in the light, like mother-of-pearl. Surely this was the vision-granting substance?

She reached out and tore off a morsel. A part of her couldn't quite believe what she was doing. She felt like a spectator at a puppet show, a witness in a dream, watching some strange, unknown heroine venture into danger. But the rest of her mind knew exactly what she was up to. She had to see the visions for herself! She gobbled up the meat –

And found herself rooted to the spot.

CHAPTER 2: THE FIRST TRIP

At first, she couldn't move. She experienced a moment of sheer terror as her body grew heavy, sinking down towards the earth the way the flesh of the mushroom sank down into her belly. Would her toes become fibrous and seek out the shelter of the soil, just like those of her great-great-great grandfather?

A bitter aftertaste crawled in her throat like a horde of insects. Then her skin started crawling as well, prickling in undulating patterns, as if a host of tiny spiders were dancing all over it. Her stomach felt queasy, then buoyant, like a hot-air balloon. Her limbs felt light and airy, like a bird's hollow bones. The feeling made her laugh with excitement – and relief.

Finding she could move after all, she took a misguided step. It seemed like a very lengthy stride, but at the same time barely a shuffle. Her dress brushed her legs like something foreign. Her skin felt foreign, too, clammy and crawling but airy and free. The contours of the air seemed to warp and the shapes of the trees rippled like a summer horizon. Was her vision beginning?

Steadily, the clearing became a kaleidoscope. Gouts of rainbow fire began to crawl across her mind's open eye, repainting the sky in hues of pink and orange. The air shimmered in a curtain of colour. She took a faltering step, pushed through it –

And emerged somewhere else entirely.

Whoa…

The garden had gone. It its place celestial vistas shone down through a web woven from tendrils of fungus with pulses of light shooting through them. Each circular gap in the web offered a window to some other sky. Through one of the windows could be seen a riot of nebulas and stars; through another came a slice of bright sunlight, so that night and day intertwined with one another in some transcendental tapestry.

At length she took her eyes off the multiform sky. The ground beneath her feet was fibrous and runnelled, like a giant-sized version of the disembodied brain one of her tutors kept in a jar of preservative fluids on his desk. Otherwise it looked like the flesh of a mushroom.

Ziqqora paused and took a very deep breath. It felt healthy and clear. Gone was the nausea she'd experienced earlier. Her whole being felt light. Her skin seemed to glow, so too her golden hair. She looked at her palms; they were no longer grazed or dirty from her fall into the garden. She felt no hunger, no tiredness, no discomfort at all. Was she even awake? Had she been transported in spirit? Perhaps she was *dead!*

She looked around again. A solitary landmark rose in the distance, a monolithic structure of imposing black stone. Having no other destination, she set off towards it. The sight of it worked some kind of magick on her mind, stirring up something she couldn't quite place, something very intimate and deep, like a reoccurring dream or a memory from childhood obscured by the passage of time. A sense of eerie familiarity gripped her. Did she know of this place, somewhere deep down, or was it just the locus of some spiritual gravity that felt intimate to everyone? There were such places, she knew, though she'd only ever seen them in dreams.

As she crept through the arches of the building, she almost said "Hello? Is anyone there?" But the place seemed too quiet to disturb with any sound, so she went on quietly, her steps light and airy but echoing anyway.

The interior was very nearly empty, save for a statue glowing with some indwelling radiance. It depicted a massive and blossoming flower. Lounging in its centre, as if upon a bed, was a naked and beautiful woman. Her face was completely covered by locks of falling hair, and her legs were spread wide open, revealing her pussy, so that her posture and anatomy mimicked the bloom of the flowerbed she sat in. Ziqqora felt a tingle between her own legs, not because she found the statue sexy, but because the image called out to her on some other level, exuding a presence of raw sensuality.

For a while, she just stood frozen before it, staring.

Then she heard footsteps behind her.

CHAPTER 3: THE DEMON'S DREAM

Ziqqora spun to see a figure in the shadows just beyond the statue's light. It looked vaguely like a man, but his body was seething and as-yet-unformed, like a cloud of fungal spores taking shape and congealing. She felt a pulse of fear, and backed towards the statue.

"Don't be afraid," said the stranger.

He stepped into the light, young, handsome, and dressed in regal garments.

"Hi," he said. "My name's Mycoz. What's yours?"

Ziqqora was speechless for a moment. Then she managed to stammer her name.

"We haven't had a visitor like you in a while," he said. "Do you know where you are?"

She shook her head.

"We're in my father's dream," he said.

Ziqqora just stood there, wide-eyed.

"Let me try and clarify," he said, noting her confusion. "It all starts with my grandmother. That's her statue right behind you."

Ziqqora turned back towards the image, noting the woman's nubile figure and beautiful features.

"Pretty foxy for a granny," she whispered.

Mycoz smiled. "She's a full-blooded demon. They don't really age like you or I do."

Ziqqora's eyes lit up with wonder. She'd learned of many demons from her tutors – their names, their passions, their predilections and predations. Perhaps she'd learned of this one, as well?

"A demon?" she asked. "What's her name?"

"She doesn't have one," he said, sadly. "Not anymore. The other demons took it, flayed it from her soul, like skin from a body."

"Why?"

"You know about the Cosmic War, right? The Great Deicide?"

Ziqqora nodded. Again, thanks to her tutors, she knew about both events. Apparently, the universe had once been ruled by things called gods, but the demons had killed them all long, long ago. Then they'd unleashed the pure essence of Chaos at the heart of creation, a substance called Celestial Fire, which burned down the cosmos and created it anew, ushering in the present cycle of time and existence: the Aeon of Chaos. The whole story was vague, full of holes and contradictions, but it *had* provided excellent fodder for Ziqqora's many daydreams.

"My gran there was one of the god-killers," said Mycoz. "But, sometime after the Deicide, she and some friends of hers had the bright idea of trying to be deities themselves. So they formed into a faction and started doing what gods used to do – demanding worship and sacrifice, binding mortals into webs of cruel Fate, that sort of thing. They even inspired the creation of an empire to venerate them. The place was called Ozich. Heard of it?"

"Of course," she said. Her tutors had told her about Old

Ozich, too, not that there'd been much to tell. The empire had sprung up and spread out like wildfire, then suddenly collapsed almost five hundred years ago. Its monuments were almost all gone. The only real relic of its presence was the language it had spread across the continents, which Ziqqora and Mycoz were speaking right now.

"The other demons got upset, obviously," he said. "They'd fought pretty hard to rid the universe of gods, and they didn't want their efforts being wasted. A schism erupted between the demons of Ozich and those who were loyal to the cause of the Deicide. It turned into a full-blown civil war. Eventually my gran's faction lost. Their punishment was terrible. First their names were taken. Then their incarnations were sundered from their oversouls and sent into exile. Only one of them escaped."

"Who?"

"My dad. He was incarnate as a mushroom when they caught him, so he abandoned his flesh and put his soul into a spore cloud. He drifted on the winds for a while, then fell into a valley and seeped into the soil. He didn't stop until he landed in a chasm, deep below the earth, where he started regrowing. Eventually his tendrils shot up through the ground. I'll spare you the lurid details, but demons are randy by nature, it seems, so he ended up mating with a lot of the locals. Local fungi, that is. That's how myself and my siblings got made."

Ziqqora's eyes went wide.

"You're a...a mushroom?" she asked, staring at his handsome and very human-looking features.

"Half-mushroom," he corrected. "My physical body isn't all that ambulatory most of the time. But my soul is free to come and go as it pleases. So is yours, now that you've eaten of my flesh."

"Your flesh*?"*

"Yep," said Mycoz, smiling.

She stared at him, trying to reconcile the giant, technicolour toadstool with the being that stood before her. She felt more than a little perturbed. The groundskeeper had been correct; the 'shrooms really did harbour inhuman intelligence. She was speaking with one of those intellects right now. Would he punish her for eating his flesh? Would he bind her body to the earth in the form of a mushroom, while trapping her soul in this place?

Or perhaps he'd make her his concubine. Sexual images flickered through her mind – her white thighs spread wide around his heaving, grinding hips; his prick spearing deeply inside of her. It was a sensation she'd often imagined, but had never truly known. The closest she'd come was with the probings of her own slender fingers. Would he be gentle, she wondered – or rough? Would his lust even know any limits? Would be plunder her body, one hole after another?

She started getting wet in spite of her terror. But why was she finding such hideous prospects arousing? Why was she even imagining them at all? She felt the heat of the statue behind her, pulsing, seething, as though it were in tune with her own frantic blood.

This thing's messing with my head! she thought, and pulled away from the image, even though her movements took her closer to the demon-spawn.

The haze of lust dissipated. The sexual images faded from her eyes, whirling off into blackness. She glanced at the statue, warily. Mycoz chuckled.

"They called her the Queen of the Carnal Garden," he said. "Her image still seems to have a stirring effect. My dad keeps it here for sentimental reasons, to remember what she used to be like, before her mutilation."

Ziqqora stared at him. He still seemed quite gentlemanly. But was his seeming sincere, or merely a charade? Would his flesh peel off into a cloud of mushroom spores and start invading her airways? Would her body be mutated, her soul made a prisoner?

She took a deep breath. This torture of uncertainty had to end, one way or another.

"My ancestors used to come here," she said. "Then my great-great-great grandfather got turned into a mushroom. People think he was cursed, but no one really knows what happened."

"And you want to find out?"

She nodded.

He smiled. "Why don't you come and ask him yourself?"

She followed him out into the scintillating landscape. At first they were the only ones there. Then a series of shapes began to fall from the portals that filled up the sky. They looked a bit like comets, with inchoate bodies of quicksilver brightness. Ziqqora watched in amazement as they came to a sudden, floating stop just above the squishy earth, and began to transform before her eyes.

One became an orb of floating fire; another became crystalline, reflecting the light of the heavens through the facets of its body; another was a silent incarnation of lightning, with fingers that flickered and streaked; another was a gigantic crocodile with eyes that extruded on stalks and blinked with lids like the petals of carnivorous flowers.

Fuck!

Ziqqora shrieked and backed away.

"Fallon!" snapped Mycoz. "Stop messing with our guest, you little jerk!"

The crocodile transformed into the likeness of a cute young boy and stuck out his tongue. Then another light descended, taking the shape of a man in his prime. He wore royal robes of myriad colours and his head was encircled by a crown. Ziqqora looked at him with wide-open eyes. His image was one she'd passed many times in the palace, painted in oils and hung up on the walls. It was Boletus, her great-great-great grandfather, the last of the Mushroom Kings. His features looked a little like hers.

"You appear rather familiar, young lady," he said. "Am I detecting a family resemblance?"

"I'm your great-great-great granddaughter, Ziqqora."

"Ha! I was wondering when my descendants would turn up to visit me. It seems like an awfully long time. I thought maybe they'd forgotten…"

"They thought you were dead. Cursed into the shape of a mushroom."

"Whatever gave them that idea?"

"You did. I mean, you literally turned into a mushroom."

"That's because I wanted to live here, instead! I'm afraid I might've left the kingdom in a bit of disarray, but it was just so dreadfully *dull*. It's much more fun here, in the Demon's Dream, and the many realms beyond it. Come to think of it, I've got a date with a hot young demoness near the Maw of

Cassiopion. Goodbye for now, my dear!"

"Wait!"

But he was already transforming back into a comet and shooting up into the sky, where he vanished through one of the portals. The rest of the figures departed in similar style. It seemed that they too had better ways to spend their time.

What the fuck? was the sum of the thoughts that Ziqqora could muster.

Mycoz laughed. "That ancestor of yours is incorrigible!" he said.

"So he wasn't cursed at all," she whispered, talking more to herself than to anyone else. "He *decided* to stay here…"

"That's right," said Mycoz. "You see, my family and yours made a pact long ago. They'd guard our bodies in the waking world. In exchange, we'd let them eat of our flesh and come visit us here."

"*Here,*" she said. "Meaning your father's dream…?"

"That's right. He's sleeping under the earth, waiting for a time to re-emerge. But his mind is like a realm unto itself. It's connected to many other places by the gates you see above you. Sort of like a crossroads, but with a whole lot of forks. Anyone who comes here can make use of the portals to travel all over the cosmos. That's what your ancestors did. They travelled through the gateways in their spirit bodies, getting all sorts of knowledge that helped them run their kingdom. But it seems like someone made a mess of things and forgot to pass on the secrets of this place, which means we haven't had a guest like you in a while now. Which is a shame, really. I rather liked hanging around with humans. Still, better late than never, right?"

Ziqqora nodded, then paused. The way he'd been talking, it sounded as if he'd borne witness to all of those events first hand.

"Just how old are you?" she asked.

He shrugged. "Time's a bit slippery here," he said. "It is a dream, after all. And time passes differently in other realms, as well. Would you like to explore a few?" Smiling politely, he offered her his hand.

She paused for a moment. But what was the danger? His family and hers were allies of old. Her great-great-great grandfather hadn't been cursed with the shape of a mushroom – he'd become that way willingly. What's more, the Demon's Dream was exciting, wilder than her wildest daydreams.

She smiled and put her hand in his, then bid farewell to the earth beneath her feet.

CHAPTER 4: STAR QUEST

The sensation of flying was somewhat like falling asleep, when she'd feel her consciousness unmooring from her body and drifting away, except that this time her body came with her.

They drifted up light as the air. At first Mycoz was pulling her, like some runaway kite, but then she started floating on her own, as if the only thing holding her down had been some stubborn superstition of gravity, and now it was gone.

The two of them flew up through a portal and emerged above a blood-red sea filled with giant white lampreys. The creatures were bigger than ships, bigger than whales. They seemed to be feeding on something even bigger, something whose shadow filled the deep like a great sunken continent. They writhed in their multitudes around it, occasionally breaking the surface in explosions of spume, then diving back down again. Suddenly one of them leapt very high. For a terrible moment Ziqqora thought it might keep ascending and swallow her and Mycoz whole with its hideous circular maw. A tremor of dread ran through her, even as the beast fell back down into the waters.

"Don't worry," said Mycoz, who must've felt her hand trembling in his. "We're here in spirit form. Very few things have the power to hurt us – especially not these things."

Ziqqora made herself calm down. Steadily her fear gave way to a sense of pure exhilaration as they flew on above the blood-red sea. In the distance she saw islands of onyx dotted with lighthouse-like obelisks blasting out beams of revolving blue light. When they struck her, they filled her with the dreams of dead sailors. Some were bittersweet with nostalgia; others were raunchy fantasies of lovers and prostitutes in port. The lust she felt was alien, anatomically-speaking, but otherwise familiar. It hit her with the force of the blood-scented winds that whipped above the great gruesome sea. For a moment she was paralysed by the intensity. Then Mycoz pulled on her hand, and they flitted back though the portal, through the Demon's Dream, and out into a starscape.

They strode along a road made of meteoric dust, even though they didn't need to walk. Ziqqora spied a human-like body in the distance. The size of a planetoid, its own gravitational force had screwed up its limbs into a ball, so that it hovered in the heavens in the posture of a foetus, even though it looked like a bearded old man. Its blood had been frozen into icicles that drifted around it like satellites. They looked like giant snowflakes, albeit glittering and red.

Must be one of the old, dead god-things, thought Ziqqora.

She knew from her lessons that most had been devoured by the demons or burnt by Celestial Fire, but some of their bodies were still floating in the void. Sometimes their bones or their calcified organs would fall down to earth like meteors, exploding. Their black metal bones were much prized among royals. Her own father had a sliver of god-bone that served as a dagger.

A huge, vague shape came swimming through the blackness. She saw it at first as an absence of stars in the distance, drawing closer and closer, not to them but to the carcass. Ziqqora couldn't stop herself from shaking as she saw it more clearly, even though she knew it probably couldn't sense them. She found herself huddling close to Mycoz, trying to shelter in his presence. He clustered close to her, too. Was that a shiver she felt, running though his frame? Even he was afraid of it!

The thing looked like a giant maggot, fat and long, so big it made her feel vertigo. She didn't understand how she hadn't seen it sooner. Something as big as that, against the star-strewn blanket of space, should've been visible for many miles. And yet it had emerged from the darkness like a shark from the depths. Perhaps it had its own means of slipping in and out from underneath the skin of the void? Either way, it was out of hiding now, and hungry. It tore into the dead god's body with gusto, slurping down the meat. Its pale body pulsated, like a wineskin getting fuller.

"The demon worm, Krauwm," said Mycoz with another shiver of dread.

Ziqqora knew that name; she'd also heard it in her lessons. Krauwm had started out just as an ordinary maggot; then grown bloated from consuming dead god-flesh. Since then he'd been growing and growing, feasting on the deific cadavers that floated in space, drinking their ichor and sucking their marrow. Many mortals paid homage to him, as though he were a substitute for those he'd devoured.

"We'd better get moving," Mycoz added, "in case he tries to eat us too."

"He can see us?"

"Of course he can. So can wizards and most other things with second sight. Come on!"

They flew towards a portal up ahead. Drawn by their movement, the demon worm flew after. Despite his fat frame, his speed was incredible. He shot towards them like a squid underwater. Soon his mouth gaped behind them like a hungry black star. The breath that came out was like a breeze from all the abattoirs on earth. His rows of curving teeth were bedecked with the golden skins of gods long devoured.

"Shit!" said Ziqqora.

Then the portal loomed up and swallowed them both before the Krauwm could, leaving the demon worm to snap his teeth on empty air before going back to his feast.

Ziqqora breathed a sigh of relief as they returned to the Demon's Dream. Their brush with the worm had been exciting, for sure, but also terrifying. She hoped for a more tranquil destination this time.

Through the next portal, they alighted on a ring of white dust swirling around a gas giant. Castles hung in the distance like satellites, the homes of cosmic demons who dwelt in the void.

There seemed to be a party going on in one of them. The windows strobed with psychedelic light. Music filtered out across the starscape, all beautiful and terrible at once. The vocals were a mixture of singing and wailing. No mortal man nor woman could make such a sound. The tune that went with them was nothing like the orderly melodies her father's royal minstrels often played in the palace. Wild and ever-changing, it called for a dance that didn't end. Ziqqora felt a pulse of excitement, and reached out her hand towards Mycoz, even though it was somewhat improper for a princess to do so.

"Shall we?" she asked.

Mycoz smiled and took her hand. Together they danced

around the ring of cosmic dust. The planet beside them seethed with mercury and crimson. They seemed to dance for untold hours as the demon music mutated, surging in crescendos and suddenly exploding, scattering its notes like flaming streaks of fireworks, only to gather them quickly and draw them back up again, like leaves in a whirlwind ascending. Ziqqora found herself staring deep into Mycoz's eyes. His pupils seemed to glint, as if with specks of distant starlight. His body against hers was solid and warm. The friction of their dancing was giving her a tingle, so too the sight of his face, handsome and full against the backdrop of planets and stars.

So what if he's really a mushroom? she thought.

She pulled him close, and kissed him on the lips.

And awoke a moment later, and found herself embracing the same giant toadstool she'd fed from, her lips against its technicolour skin.

She got up and glanced around. She felt like she'd been in that other place for hours, but the sun was still high in the sky, inching close to its midday meridian, as though she'd only been sleeping – or dreaming – for minutes. Her head felt peculiar, her stomach queasy. That feeling of lightness was still clinging to her limbs, but only a little bit, yielding to a growing sense of gravity and tiredness. Her thoughts felt scattered like dead autumn leaves. She tried to whip them up into coherence.

Was it all just a dream? she wondered.

But no, it couldn't have been – it was all too real! And there, standing right beside her, as tangible proof, was the mutated body of her great-great-great grandfather, his mushrooming head still adorned with a crown, while his spirit roamed the cosmos undying.

Ziqqora grinned to herself. Despite her fatigue and undeniable nausea, she still felt incredibly excited. She'd discovered the secret of the garden – and it was wondrous! She couldn't wait to tell her father the truth. Then he could eat of the mushrooms as his forefathers had, and thereby gain the knowledge he'd need to restore his kingdom's fortunes! The Mushroom Kings, long vanished from the earth, could return to Myconia, and the realm could crawl back from its state of decay!

She ran towards home with a spring in her step – over the fence, through the woods, then back across the manicured lawn that abutted the palace. She was so happy, so buoyant, she didn't even notice Bertrand, the groundskeeper's son, watching her emerge from the forest with covetous eyes.

CHAPTER 5: THE DINNER

Only a few sentries saw her as she snuck back into the palace, but Ziqqora knew they wouldn't tell. How could they, without admitting to a dereliction of duty, and thus being flogged? Sometimes her father's iron discipline had its inadvertent upsides. To her delight she found her rooms undisturbed and unattended, save for the dummy she'd left in her bed. She dismantled its body of pillows and wig, then slid beneath the sheets and lay there in daydreams till the dinner bell rang.

All too soon, she was sitting at the twenty-foot table that bisected the dining room. Her place was in the middle, opposite her stepsisters. Luckily the table was too wide for them to kick her underneath it, as she knew they would like to. Instead they just made awful faces when no one was looking, sneering and poking out their tongues at her. Then they'd turn to one another, whispering and giggling, as they presently were.

Ziqqora glared at them. They were twins with ginger hair. The freckles on their corpse-white skin looked like spots of drying blood on the faces of dead men.

Maybe it's true what they say, thought Ziqqora. *Maybe red-headed people really don't have souls!*

She knew they hated her; they said it often enough. They resented her place as the heir to the throne. So did their stepmother, who sat at the head of the table to Ziqqora's far left, though she was far more cagey than her daughters when it came to expressing her resentment. She wasn't a red-head, like them, but blond and waif-like and pretty in her way. But her blue eyes were cold, and her bosom seemed to hold all the warmth of a mortuary slab.

When I'm queen I'll banish them, thought Ziqqora.

Not to someplace awful, of course, just someplace where she wouldn't have to deal with them. Until then, she'd just have to suffer her stepsisters' mockeries, as well as their mother's false smiles and condescension. But she wouldn't let such things get her down tonight. She had important discoveries to share with her father!

Turning to him, she smiled. Her thoughts were no longer scattered. Her body was just a little bit queasy and airy, but the first few courses of dinner had helped. They'd had venison and pheasant, forcemeat of mussels and lobsters and squid, followed by duck liver paste. The wine had flowed liberally, and everyone drank, though Ziqqora, being a princess, had to take her wine with water for the sake of propriety. Still, she felt a little bit buzzed, and very, very happy. It was time to unveil her great secret!

"Dad?" she said.

Her father was bearded and greying and plump. He always smelled of sweat, but Ziqqora found the aroma somewhat comforting.

"Yes dear?" he replied.

"What do you know about the forbidden garden?" she asked, starting out coyly. "You know, the mushrooms there? Because I heard the old kings used to eat them all the time. Then they'd fly across the earth in the spirit, spying on their enemies and getting all the knowledge they needed to slaughter their foes and bring joy to the people. That's why the kingdom of Myconia used to be so powerful, isn't it? Maybe you should try eating the mushrooms too? Maybe we all should!"

She smiled excitedly, waiting for her father's response. For a moment he just sat there. Then his brows became furrowed and dark, like gathering clouds, and his cheeks reddened with anger, like the surface of a sea in which sharks have been feeding.

"Who told you that?" he hissed.

"Just a little bird," said Ziqqora, growing unsettled.

"If I ever find out who that little bird is, then I'll be sure to clip its wings, and its lying little tongue into the bargain. That garden is off-limits for a reason."

"But the old kings —"

"The old kings were fools!" he roared. "They got tricked by a demon. He lured them to his grove and gave them false visions so he could cripple their bodies and gobble up their souls. My great-grandfather himself saw the truth of this, when he beheld his own sire transformed into a travesty!"

"What if he *wanted* to be a mushroom?"

"Balderdash! Who would want to be a mushroom, a turnip, a carrot, a fucking plantain? Such is a fate worse than death. You need to get your head out of the clouds, girl."

As the king sat there seething, his wife made a disapproving noise, sucking the air through her teeth.

"I've told you time and again you need to be firmer with her," she said, speaking of Ziqqora as though she weren't there. "All she does is dream all day. No wonder she's got such silly notions in her head. She's not living in the real world at all! But someday she'll have to. Someday soon, in fact, given what's coming."

The ominous statement gave Ziqqora a nibble of panic. She turned to her father. "What's she talking about? What's coming?"

"Never mind that now," he said. "And as for the garden, you haven't been thinking about going there, have you?"

"Of course not," lied Ziqqora.

"Good. Because if I find out you have any such notions, I'll lock you in your chambers. I'll not have my daughter transformed into a mushroom and deflowered by a demon. Is that understood?"

"Yes, Father."

"Now go to your room! You need to be punished for all of this ridiculous talk."

Ziqqora got up and flounced to her room. She lay beneath the covers awake for a while, replaying the argument with her father in her mind. Eventually other thoughts began to intrude, thoughts that had been whirling around in her head, ever since she'd whirled around the ring of that planet with her arms around Mycoz. Eventually she drifted to sleep. Which was a good thing, too – she had to get up well before the sunrise if she wanted to sneak back into the garden!

＊

Bertrand's dirt-covered face peered in through the shutters at the sleeping princess, maintaining his voyeuristic vigil. She appeared to be dreaming, and pleasant dreams at that. The kind of pleasant dreams that made him wish he could creep into her room.

He too had a journey to make in the morning, though he didn't quite know the destination. He only knew he had to follow her, should she leave for the woods once again.

* * *

The king stood in his chambers, sullenly staring at the mirror. At length he locked eyes with the reflection of his wife, lying naked on the bed.

"Why did you say that at dinner?" he asked. "You almost let the cat out of the bag. You know I don't want to tell her just yet."

"Well you'll have to tell her soon," she said.

"I suppose. But I'm still not quite sure if I want to go through with it."

"You've got no choice now, Riksmund. The agreement's been made!"

She was right, of course. He'd already offered Ziqqora's hand in marriage to Heinrich Van Gruel, the Jade Prince of Pecoz. The arrangement seemed like a necessity. The kingdom of Myconia was ailing, beset from the north by the Dead Heads of Lichhelm, and menaced from the east by the young king of Yule. Their only hope of survival lay in a powerful alliance, and Heinrich Van Gruel was a powerful man – young, vigorous, and a terror on the battlefield. He was famed for his performance at the battle of Troll Tooth Pass, where, perhaps inspired by the battle's location, he'd torn out the throats of two enemy commanders with his teeth. Not because he was a maniac, of course, but because his sword had been broken, and he'd needed to improvise. His was just the sort of strength that the kingdom of Myconia now needed on its side.

And yet, there were horrible rumours about him. His family was notorious for having made some pact with a certain clan of itinerant sorcerers. His first thirteen brides had all died on their wedding nights, under unknown circumstances. For all his valiant deeds, a sinister cloud hung over the young man. King Riksmund felt sick when he thought about handing Ziqqora over to him. Not just because she was his only daughter – a fact which might make any father blanch – but because of the danger she faced. Would she end up like those other thirteen princesses, dead from some mysterious malady – or even worse, murdered?

Why the fuck did I agree to this? he wondered.

Then he glanced back at his wife, and remembered why. She'd spent the past few months persuading him in favour of the marriage by every conceivable means at her disposal. Sometimes she'd been harsh and nagging, wearing down his will the way a caustic sea breeze eats away at a mountain. Other times she'd been weepy and seemingly helpless, crying about her uncertain future. Without an alliance they were doomed, she insisted. Their kingdom would be conquered, their lands overrun. He'd be executed, or walled up in a tower; *she'd* be enslaved as a concubine and ravaged by some horny invader. Ziqqora would be ravaged, too. If he didn't give his daughter to be married, she'd be turned into a whore. Wouldn't she be far better off being wed to a prince like Van Gruel?

The queen had used other strategies, too, rendering their bed a frosty and loveless domain until the king had come around to her point of view, at which point she'd leapt upon his cock like a rabbit in heat. There were so many twists and turns to her persuasion that he felt like a leaf in a whirlwind. Right now, staring at his reflection and contemplating the fate of his daughter, he felt his inner will rise up in disgust from the core of his being, like a surging tide of vomit.

"Perhaps it's not too late to call it off," he whispered.

"Don't be ridiculous!" she shrieked.

He glared at her reflection in the mirror.

The queen stared back. She must have realised he wasn't in any mood to be bullied this night, for when she finally answered him, her voice became pleasant and soothing.

"I know you're worried," she said. "It's only natural for a father to be so. But we *need* this alliance, and the deal has been made. Van Gruel is already on his way here, Riksmund. He'll arrive in two days! If you deny him now, at this juncture, then *he'll* be our enemy, as well. He won't be able to brook such an insult. And why should he? He's a fine young man. Those awful rumours about him aren't true at all. He's just had a run of bad luck, that's all. I've got it on good authority – my cousin's an officer in his army, you know – and *he* told me that those thirteen brides all died of the plague. But Ziqqora's a healthy young thing, she'll be fine. And Van Gruel's a very handsome young man. I'm sure she'll be besotted with him. She'll be happy, he'll be happy, you'll be happy – the whole entire kingdom will be happy!"

"And so will you."

"Of course!" she said. "Your joy is mine, my beloved. Now why don't you come over here, and let me sooth that worried head of yours? You need to relieve some tension. You don't want to bank up the furnace!"

The king stood before the mirror, vacillating. He felt caught up in the whirlwind again. At length he abandoned his troubling reflection and strode to the bed. The queen crawled over to the edge with a hungry-looking smile.

***

Her mouth was full, but her eyes kept on smiling. Not because she particularly liked the feeling of his prick in her mouth, but because she knew she'd won.

She also knew the secret of Van Gruel, and the terrible rumours about him were pleasantries compared with the truth. Any woman who married him would certainly die. Which meant that in just a few days she'd be rid of her pesky little stepdaughter for good, leaving her red-headed offspring free to inherit the throne.

When Riksmund shuddered and came in her mouth she drank it down hungrily. Not because she particularly enjoyed the taste, but because the flavour of his seed had been transformed by her own deceptive alchemy. It tasted like victory.

CHAPTER 6: PREDATORS

Ziqqora got up before dawn, roused by her own urgent need to get back to the garden. She set up the dummy in her bed and snuck out across the lawn, just like she'd done the day before.

Soon, she was climbing back over the fence and into the garden. The journey felt a lot shorter this time, now she knew the way. She smiled and waved happily to her great-great-great grandfather and the rest of his court, who stood there still as statues, their sprouting bodies all dripping with spores. They didn't wave back.

Oh well, she thought. *I guess I'll see them soon enough in the spirit!*

But the person she really wanted to see was Mycoz. She found his toadstool body and took a bite of his flesh. She didn't rip it off this time, but tenderly kissed it, sucking the meat until it came loose in her mouth. *I've given him a hickey!* she thought, then felt a thrill as her body turned light once again and the air in the garden transformed into a curtain of shimmering colour. She stepped through the curtain –

And emerged into the Dream once again. There was no one there. How would she find Mycoz? Perhaps she'd go back to their very first meeting place.

She skipped with flying steps towards the monolithic building, and waited inside by the statue. Once again she felt its radiant warmth filling her body with desire. This time she luxuriated in it. It seemed like the perfect preparation for what she had in mind.

Finally, Mycoz stepped out of the shadows. For a moment his form looked unstuck, like a roiling mass of spores. Then he was handsome, and human-like, again.

"You're back!" he said with a smile.

"How could I stay away?"

"Would you like to explore a little more? Maybe visit with your ancestor?"

"Maybe later. For now, why don't we go someplace quiet, and sweet? I've got something to talk to you about."

He shrugged. "Okay. I think I've got just the place."

She took his hand and they flew up through a portal. She concentrated on his fingers intermeshed with her own. They felt warm and soft, but not nearly as clammy, nor as throbbing with blood. The excitement she felt was everywhere, flaring right out to the tips of her pinkies.

They flew down into a beautiful grove. The green of the trees was almost searingly bright, but the sunshine was soft and hung in the air like a nimbus. The ground was covered in a blanket of clover as fluffy as a featherbed.

"This is a realm of pure spirit," said Mycoz, plucking at the clover and throwing it up in the air by way of demonstration. "Everything is tangible to us."

He smiled, and Ziqqora smiled back. A current of flirtation ran between them.

"So," he said, "what'd you want to –"

Suddenly he froze, noticing something behind her. She turned to see the creature that had emerged from the undergrowth nearby. It looked like a stallion, with a coat as black as onyx and a spiralling horn atop its head. Its eyes were shining emerald, its jaws filled with fangs.

"A unicorn!" said Ziqqora.

She took a step towards it, reaching out her hand. Mycoz tried to pull her back.

"Be careful," he said. "They can –"

The unicorn nuzzled her hand. Then it grumbled at Mycoz and trotted away.

"You should look out for those," he said. "They can be dangerous. Unless you're a virgin, of course."

"They don't harm virgins?"

"No. Their father, the great demon unicorn, forbids it. He likes to deflower them himself."

"Oh," she said, contemplating this with some disquiet. Then she smiled. "It's funny the topic of virginity came up. That's sort of what I wanted to talk to you about. Well, not exactly talk…"

"Oh?" said Mycoz.

She leapt on him, kissing him and sending the both of them tumbling to the grass. When they finally broke off from their kisses Ziqqora was flushed. Mycoz looked shocked, but happy, too.

"You want to?" he asked.

She nodded. They started pulling off each other's clothing. Mycoz's garments were easy to remove, almost as if they *wanted* to come off. Ziqqora's were a little bit harder to shed. She wore voluminous layers of lace, some of them diaphanous, others opaque. They came off eventually, followed by her silken undergarments. As Mycoz undressed her she stared at his prick in wide-eyed excitement. So mesmerised she was by the sight of her lover's erection – the first of its kind she'd ever seen – that she barely even noticing when the last of her clothes had been removed, leaving her naked.

Mycoz stopped and stared at her. She lay on a bed of her own golden hair. She was nubile, and pale, and her tender skin glowed in the sunlight. Strawberry nipples poked up from her breasts.

She ogled him in turn, finally snatching her eyes from his cock. He was toned, supple, and perfectly formed. No hint of the fungal could be found in his features, except, perhaps, in the ruddy-looking tip of his erection, which bore, like all others of its ilk, a passing resemblance to the cap of a mushroom.

"Will it hurt?" she asked.

"Not in this realm," he said. "But first…"

He dove his head down between her legs.

"What're you – OH!"

Her eyes went wide with shock as he started to lick her. But the shock was ecstatic, and she threw back her head with a smile.

* * *

The princess was so excited by her journey – and whatever she planned to do – that she failed to even notice being followed as she entered the forest.

Not that Bertrand's presence was that easy to perceive. He hid behind trees and trod lightly through the undergrowth, hanging back a few dozen feet. Sometimes he lost sight of her completely, but he'd participated in more than a few royal hunts in a servant's capacity, and knew well how to follow the tracks of his prey.

He didn't exactly like the look of the place, this garden. The forms of the mushrooms were unsettling. Some looked like claws reaching up from the earth, others like corrugated brain-tissue. He'd heard all the stories from his father, about how the mushrooms were home to some terrible intelligence, and took vengeance on those who consumed or abused them.

But Bertrand didn't care. His desire for the princess was stronger than fear. He'd spied through her shutters every night since he'd first felt a tingle downstairs. He'd wanked himself raw to those memories more times than he could count. He knew she didn't like him, of course, but he didn't much care about that either.

He found her alone in a grove, save for the presence of several hideous figures resembling mushroom-men. At first they gave him pause, but he pressed on regardless. She was lying on the ground beside a gigantic toadstool, seemingly sleeping. Her clothes were disarrayed, her cheeks flushed, her languid face smiling with lust unmistakable.

Was she having a sex dream, he wondered? Or had she noticed him following after all, and therefore decided to play some sort of game with him?

Either way he didn't mind. He crept up beside her, knelt, and pulled up her dress, bunching it up on her stomach as he stared at her undergarments. They were made from white silk. A spot of dark moisture was present at the crotch. He knelt down and sniffed it, growing even more aroused as he did so. It was the very same perfume he'd smelt many times when he'd stolen such items from the castle laundry, but this time it was fresh.

He struggled to calm himself as he set about pulling her shoes off and dragging down her drawers. The hem slid off her waist and her pubes began to slowly appear, bushy and golden in the sunlight. He tugged even harder, yearning to see what lay lower. At long last her pussy appeared, albeit compact and hidden by the slope of her body and the press of her thighs. Smiling and fondling himself, he began to advance.

* * *

Ziqqora lay back moaning, writhing her thighs around My-coz's head and gripping his hair in her hands. Shockwaves of pleasure rippled out from the touch of his tongue as it lapped her. The air became shimmering and rippling and bright. She was headed for a climax unlike any she'd given herself in the past. She gripped his head tightly, seizing, bracing herself –

When the sensation suddenly changed.

* * *

Bertrand spread her legs and stared down at the lips of her pussy. He was about to get closer when he heard something stirring behind him, and turned to see tendrils shooting up from the soil near the toadstool.

His eyes went wide. He froze for a second that seemed like a minute, watching the pads of the tendrils uncoil, dripping with fluid and filled with little fleshy proboscises that looked almost like nipples, and almost like jointless grasping fingers. They lashed out like whips, seizing his limbs and hoisting him up off the ground.

For a moment he hung there. Then came a sudden, almost incomprehensible motion, wet and hot and ravaging. He found himself spinning through the air like a top. As he landed he realised that something was very, very wrong. Most of his body hadn't come with him. His torso was slumped on the ground, armless and legless. His terrified consciousness dwelled in his own severed head – but not for very long. He tried to scream, but could only spin his eyes in their sockets as the tendrils came and got him again, pulling his parts into the moist black soil.

* * *

"Why'd you stop?" asked Ziqqora.

Mycoz smiled up at her, his mouth smeared with wet.

"Sorry," he said. "There was a disturbance in the garden that I had to take care of. Now, where was I?"

He dove back between her legs and resumed his ministrations. She felt the pleasure start to build once again, then suddenly explode to the rhythm of the colours that flashed before her eyes. He drew back, smiling, with even wetter lips.

"Now?" he asked.

She closed her eyes and nodded, waiting.

Her eyes flew open wide as he entered. Once more the shock was exquisite, but a thousand times greater. He hadn't been lying when he said there'd be no pain in this place. All that she felt was the pleasure of sweet penetration, growing greater and greater with each spearing motion.

She lay back for a time, trembling and murmuring, overwhelmed by the novel sensation. Then she got in on the movements, bucking her hips and rising up to meet him. They sat in the lotus position, her arms around his neck, his hands on her hips and her rump, lifting her bright, airy body.

They bounced and rocked and eventually flew up into the air, their limbs intertwisted, their senses exploding as their mutual pleasure kept mounting in tune with their ascent. She let out a moan as an orgasm gripped her like a hand of benevolent lightning, then sent her spinning into freefall in the aftermath. Mycoz held her tightly and hammered even harder, a crescendo of movement that ended with a climax of his own. He shuddered and slowed as his seed spurted into her. They wriggled together, teasing out the last of it, then fluttered to the earth like a pair of gentle leaves, landing in the clover. He pulled out his prick with a slippery motion. Their juices dribbled between them.

"Will I get pregnant?" she asked.

Mycoz laughed. "Not in this place," he said.

She smiled, then leaned in to kiss him again.

❋ ❋ ❋

This time she awoke beside the toadstool with her clothes in disarray. Her dress was bunched up on her stomach, and her garments had been pulled down beneath.

Did I do that, she wondered, *during the vision?*

She glanced around. There was a splatter of blood on the ground, all but soaked into the soil. Perhaps it was hers? She had just lost her virginity, after all. She slipped a finger inside herself, probing. It still felt very tight; she could barely proceed past the knuckle. Nor was any blood on her finger as she slipped it back out again, only the shimmer of her juices in the sun.

Guess I'm still a virgin after all, she thought. *In the physical world, at least!*

She glanced back at the blood. Perhaps a wounded animal had limped through the garden?

Who cares? she thought.

She ran towards home with a spring in her step. The sun was still at the zenith of noon, even though they'd made love for what'd seemed like many hours, over and over again, trying out a myriad of positions both floating and grounded.

Time can be slippery here, he'd said.

Clearly he was right! Soon she arrived back at the palace, crept to her room, and breathed out a sigh of relief as she saw that the dummy was still undisturbed in her bed. She put the dummy away and slipped back beneath the covers, lounging in a post-coital haze until the dinner-bell rang.

This time she stayed quiet about the garden. Perhaps she'd try talking to her father again sometime in the future, when he wasn't being quite so pig-headed, and perhaps, more importantly, when her stepmother wasn't in the room. For now she was happy to keep it her own little secret. And what a secret it was! She tried not to giggle and blush during the first seven courses of dinner. Even the scowls of her stepsisters couldn't dampen her mood. She was in love! Or maybe just in lust, assuming that those things were even different at all. Either way it felt pretty good. It seemed like nothing could impinge upon her happiness – until her father made his announcement.

"Ziqqora," he said, "I've got some news that concerns you."

"Oh?" She glanced up, suddenly worried her earlier excursion had been noticed after all.

"You're going to be married."

"To who?" she asked, too shocked to really process his words. She'd always known this day would come, but it had always felt like a faraway thing, like death, or old age, or the end of the world.

"To Heinrich Van Gruel, the Jade Prince of Pecoz."

Ziqqora froze. She'd heard all about the Jade Prince. His thirteen brides had all died on their wedding nights in sinister circumstances.

"But…but he's a murderer!" she said. "He kills all his wives, right after he deflowers them! Everyone knows about it!"

Her stepsisters started laughing. "You're gonna get murdered!" they said, chanting as one. "Murdered, murdered, murdered —"

"Silence!" snapped the queen. "No one's getting murdered. Those are all just vicious lies. Prince Heinrich is a marvellous man who's just had a run of bad luck, that's all. His thirteen wives all died from the plague."

"Isn't that a bit unlikely?" said Ziqqora. "Dad, you can't be serious!"

"It's all taken care of, my dear," he said. "Van Gruel's already on his way. The wedding will take place the day after tomorrow. Besides, your mother's right."

"She's not my mother!"

"She is by law! And Heinrich really is a splendid young man. I'm sure he'll care for you all the more, given the tragic manner in which his other brides have died."

Ziqqora started sobbing. "This is fucked!" she cried.

"I told you she wouldn't be able to handle it like a grownup," said her stepmother.

"You're loving this, aren't you, you fucking cunt?" snapped Ziqqora.

"That's ENOUGH!" shouted the king. "Ziqqora, go to your room and pull yourself together. We'll talk more tomorrow."

Ziqqora stormed from the dining hall and ran to her chambers, hearing her stepsisters giggling as she went. She crawled beneath the covers and wept even more. What a revolting development! It was bad enough that she had to get married to a stranger, but to a murderous maniac as well?

She had to do something, but what? Perhaps the mushroom

visions would show her the answer. She tossed and turned, doing her best to get to sleep so she could get up in the morning and make it to the garden unobserved.

Eventually she fell into a pit of fitful dreams. Thus she was well and truly dead to the world by the time a pair of figures crept into her room, holding something shiny and sharp.

CHAPTER 7: THE TWINS

Ziqqora's stepsisters stood in the darkness in front of her bed, each of them holding a pair of sharp scissors. They'd been planning on snipping off her golden locks and giving her a boy's haircut, so she'd be humiliated on the fast-approaching day of her wedding. As it was, they stood there frozen, scissors in hand, listening.

Ziqqora, it seemed, had the habit of talking in her sleep, especially when she was agitated. She must have dreamt she was arguing with her father, trying to make him see reason and call off her marriage to Van Gruel. She told him all about a garden, and her secret lover Mycoz, who was part demon, part mushroom.

"You think it's true?" whispered Rudya, the older of the pair by a few short minutes.

"If it is, we can get her in a lot of trouble," said Gyara. "No one's allowed to go into the garden."

Rudya's eyes lit up as she considered for a moment all the cruel possibilities of such a situation.

"I've got a better idea," she said.

Then she whispered into her younger sister's ear. The two of them giggled, and went off to bed.

The next morning, they were waiting when Ziqqora set off towards the forest. They followed after, wearing cowls to cover their bright red hair, and hiding their skinny bodies in the bushes whenever possible. They had some deal of trouble getting over the spiked iron fence, but they finally managed to clamber up a tree and leap over the top, tumbling into the grass on the other side. Then they followed Ziqqora's footsteps down a road of white-capped mushrooms. They found her passed out in a grove beside a gigantic toadstool. Grinning, they reached beneath their cloaks and pulled out a pair of hefty hatchets, as identical as they were.

"Which one do you think is her boyfriend?" asked Gyara.

"Not sure," whispered Rudya.

They moved around, looking at the legions of fungi filling the garden.

"What about this one?" asked Gyara as she stopped by the one closest to Ziqqora's sleeping body and raised her hatchet.

"Don't be silly," said Rudya. "That's just a giant toadstool! How could she have screwed that? It doesn't even have a thingy!"

"It looks like one big thingy to me."

"Sure, but there's no way she could fit all that inside of her."

"Maybe she sat right on top of it?"

The twins shrugged. Ziqqora's dream-talk had been somewhat vague and hard to decipher. All they knew was that she had a lover in this garden, a being that was part fungus, part demon, with the appearance of both mushroom and man.

"It's gotta be one of these," said Rudya, pointing at the mushroom-men from the old king's court.

"She had sex with *that?*" said Gyara. "Gross!"

They stared for a moment at the fungus that bore the vestigial shape of a man. Then Rudya stuffed the hatchet under her arm and tore off the thing's rotting trousers. There, between its legs, was a mess of pubes that looked like sprouts and a cock that bore the likeness of a toadstool, dripping out spore-juice from its tip. On the figure's face was a look of frozen ecstasy.

"Check out his O-face," said Rudya. "I bet she's been sucking on his thing!"

"What a dirty bitch!"

"Well she's gonna have to get a new boyfriend to blow, 'cause it's time to make mushroom salad!"

Laughing with glee, they took their hatchets and started chopping up the mushroom-man. They hacked off his flaring, spindly fingers; they chopped off his toadstool-shaped prick; they even struck deep into the flesh of his chest, finding it sloughing and moist beneath their blades.

So busy they were with their chopping and giggling, at first they didn't notice the mushroom-man's change of expression, his face twisting into a semblance of anger. Before they could even stop laughing, a mass of black spores erupted from his chest. It covered them all over, entering their nostrils, their mouths, their lungs, even their pores. The stuff was cloying and thick. It stank like a handkerchief filled with old cum. They coughed and shrieked and fled from the garden, dropping their hatchets as they went.

✳ ✳ ✳

Meanwhile, inside the Demon's Dream again, Ziqqora wrapped her arms around Mycoz, distraught.

"What's wrong?" he asked.

"It's terrible!" she cried. "I just found out I'm going to get married, to Heinrich Van Gruel! There're awful rumours about him. His first thirteen wives all died on their wedding nights. People say he murdered them! My stepmother made up some bullshit story about them all dying of the plague, but I can tell it's a lie. I bet she's behind this whole thing. She wants me to marry Van Gruel so he'll kill me, and she's tricked my dumb dad into going along with it. That cow wants me dead, just like I knew she always did!"

Ziqqora wept. In the Demon's Dream, her tears shone like silver. Mycoz wiped them away.

"Calm down," he said.

"How can I? The wedding's tomorrow. He's riding to Myconia right now!"

"Right. But there's no point getting upset until we know what we're dealing with. You said it yourself, all this stuff about Van Gruel's just rumours. So, why don't we find out the truth for ourselves??"

"We can do that?" she asked, drying her eyes.

"How else do you think your ancestors built their kingdom from nothing? By spying on their enemies."

"Through the portals!"

"Exactly. Now come on, let's go have a look-see."

Ziqqora nodded sharply. Suddenly she felt a great deal less helpless.

"How do we find him?" she asked.

"The same way an eagle finds a hare. Come on!"

They took flight, and Mycoz guided them both through one of the portals. Ziqqora found herself staring down in shock at her very own kingdom of Myconia. For some reason the sight of such a familiar place from such a high altitude was even stranger to her eyes than the cosmic vistas she'd seen on her previous trip. She saw her family's crumbling palace below, bordered by the sprawling forest to the south. She could even see the garden and its grove, peeking through a gap in the trees. The toadstools looked like daubs of kaleidoscopic colour. Was that her own sleeping body, lying next to Mycoz? It was an eerie feeling, beholding her flesh as she travelled in the spirit.

They flew on above the castle and peered out across the landscape. Beyond the wide palace moat was the city of Myconia, sprawling and crumbling in every direction. Further to the north lay the city of Lichhelm, to the east the Troll Tooth Passes, which led in turn to the kingdom of Yule. To the west was the realm of Pecoz. All had once been under Myconian rule, either as tributaries or actual dominions. Then her great-great-great grandfather had transformed into a mushroom, beginning the kingdom's long decline. The realm had shrivelled into itself, retreating from its borders and allowing new powers to rise in its wake. The whole process reminded her of that god-thing she'd seen in the void, crushed into the posture of a foetus by its own morbid gravity. She knew now the reason why her ancestors' efforts had been so completely undone: her family had forsaken the garden, and turned from the path of the Mushroom.

"Which way's he coming from?' asked Mycoz.

"West," said Ziqqora.

She took the lead, squeezing his hand as she flew. The warmth of his fingers was comfort indeed, as was the beauteous view. They passed over the dense, crowded city, where each and every building took on the likeness of a doll house and smoke rose from chimneys to fog up the sky all around them; over the paddocks and cultivated fields, where sheep lay like puffs of white wool on a blanket; over the dense, verdant forests, where the treetops rose and fell like the waves of some vast, frozen ocean. They saw children playing, lovers fucking, horsemen riding.

"There!" she cried.

Speeding through the forest was a convoy heading fast for Myconia. She'd very nearly missed it, for the whole train was decked out in livery of jade, which in the context of the wood served them almost as camouflage.

"The Jade Prince," she said. "That must be him!"

They flew lower, above the road, and peered down at the convoy, witnessing a spectacle of luxury and power with few parallels in this part of the world. The jade-coloured coaches were lacquered and shining, painted with the image of a serpent with gemstones for eyes. The horses were black, with jade-coloured tack. The knights were bedecked with jade-painted armour and surcoats of brocaded silk. At the front of the train rode a tall, handsome man on a mighty white stallion, his raven-dark hair flapping wild in the wind. It could only be Heinrich Van Gruel, the Jade Prince of Pecoz.

"He's pretty good-looking," said Mycoz. "And he's got quite a codpiece!"

Ziqqora stared down at her bridegroom's groin, where sat the biggest codpiece she'd seen in her life. Van Gruel's build was massive, but even on his muscular frame the codpiece still seemed ungainly, like some kind of prop in a theatrical comedy. Was this some peculiar Pecoz fashion, or did Van Gruel have a monster in his trousers that needed such a copious compartment?

Mycoz laughed. "At least you won't have to worry about your husband being poorly-hung!"

Ziqqora glanced at him, wondering how he could be so completely carefree. Shouldn't he be jealous that his lover was about to be taken by another? Then again, he was a demon-spawned mushroom who'd lived for untold ages in a realm where time itself seemed elastic. He might've been *her* first lover, but she doubted very much she'd been his. How many women had he known across the ages? How many mushrooms? From what she'd seen so far, the Demon's children were shape-shifters, at least when they travelled in the spirit. There was no limit to the places Mycoz had gone, the beings he'd consorted with across the dimensions. He'd probably done it with everything – animal, mineral, vegetable – alien!

They followed Van Gruel as he sped through the forest. Ziqqora began to feel in two minds about him. He was certainly the most beautiful, powerful man she'd ever seen. But, there were the deaths of his brides to consider, not to mention the size of his codpiece, which was distinctly alarming. Perhaps he'd skewered them to death on the marriage bed?

At length the convoy came to a stop beside a stream. Van Gruel leapt down, strode over to the water, and began to undress.

"Here we go," said Mycoz. "Now you'll get a really good look at him."

Ziqqora watched with unblinking eyes. First he took off his tunic and belt, revealing a sculpted chest with a rug of black hair. His muscles bulged and flexed with every subtle movement. He had the definition of a racehorse, with power to match. Ziqqora felt a tingle of undeniable desire as she watched him. Then he took off his trousers, and her eyes went wide with terror.

His cock broke free from the codpiece like a jack-in-a-box,

flailing and hissing. It wasn't a normal male organ at all, but a scaly, fanged serpent!

"Oh shit!" she said.

"Well, this isn't good," said Mycoz, showing a talent for understatement.

CHAPTER 8: THE JADE PRINCE OF PECOZ

"Down!" growled Heinrich as his serpentine member unfurled.

It hissed and bit him on the hand. He growled and shook blood from the wound. He didn't have to be concerned about the venom, of course; he was quite immune. It was more about the principle of the thing. The creature that lived between his legs just didn't obey him. It'd been that way for as long as he could remember. Not that the creature had always been with him, of course. But his memory didn't stretch back that far; he'd only been a newborn when they'd joined it to his body.

The kingdom of Pecoz had been weak back then, and his parents had needed a powerful heir. So they'd made a pact with the Sebeks, sorcerous drifters who'd fallen on hard times of their own.

For generations the Sebeks had wandered the coastlines, selling their magick to sailors. For a not inconsiderable fee they'd cast their spells and bring forth favourable winds for their clients. Those who paid them reached their destinations quickly and safely. Those who didn't often fell victim to shipwreck. Eventually people figured out the obvious truth: the Sebeks were extortionists. They weren't just casting their spells for those who paid the fees, they were summoning tempests to destroy those who didn't. Thousands had died and many fortunes had been lost because of their sorcery. The outcry against them was savage. They were lynched, or stoned, or burned at the stake wherever they were found. The few that survived fled to Pecoz, offering their magick in exchange for protection.

The Gruels took them up on it, swore a pact, and appointed the Sebeks as sorcerers to the crown. Their first task? To infuse the infant Heinrich with incredible power. In a secret ritual they sliced off his member, called forth this creature from Beyond, and grafted it forever to the stump of his manhood. Heinrich always winced when he imagined that moment, even though he couldn't remember it. Still he felt like the pain was imprinted on his mind somehow, like a bad dream after waking.

In many ways, the ritual had worked. The power of the creature suffused his flesh, and Heinrich grew up to be as strong as an ox, as swift as a fox, and as healthy as a horse. He never got sick, needed very little sleep, and was a terror on the battlefield, slaughtering the enemies of Pecoz and expanding its dominion. But the magick had its drawbacks, as well. The creature had grown up just as he had, until finally reaching its present, ungainly size. It had also grown more and more unmanageable, and had forced him to do terrible things. *It* was the reason why his thirteen young brides had all died. Heinrich had tried to resist it, but the process was nigh-on impossible. Not only did the beast have a mind of its own, but the pleasures it offered were great. Heinrich had found himself crippled by ecstasy even as he'd shuddered in horror at the deeds of the thing between his legs. Thus his relationship with the creature was deeply ambivalent. He despised its excesses, but needed the pleasures it gave. He needed its cooperation, too, but the monster was fickle indeed.

"Why did you bite me, you unruly bastard?" he hissed.

Because I don't like being locked up in the codpiece, it said, speaking directly into his mind with a sibilant voice. *It's musty and dark in there. How would you like it, being cooped up all day with a miasma of ball sweat?*

"You can't come out all the time," he whispered. "You know that. People just wouldn't understand…"

We'll make them understand! said the serpent. *Just let me hang freely. Then, as soon as someone complains about it, or makes a nasty face, or whatever, then here's what we do: you just rip off their head with that incredible strength of yours, and I'll fuck them in the neck-stump while everyone's watching. Now who else would gripe after that? Besides, you know you'd enjoy it. There's nothing like a nice, tight throat-hole, all bubbling with blood…*

Heinrich shook his head. "You have to stay in hiding, at least for the while."

Spoilsport! Coward! Loser! griped the snake.

"Enough!" shouted Heinrich. "Besides, how can I trust you with any independence after what happened last time? You promised not to hurt that girl. You promised not to hurt any of them."

I couldn't help it! Those parts they have inside of them are so soft and springy. The feel between my teeth…!

The serpent whirled in the air, flickering its tongue and gnashing its fangs in a show of excitement.

"Calm yourself," said Heinrich, even as he felt the same pulse of desire.

You know you love it, too.

"I don't," he said, lying. "And it has to stop, you hear? You've already chewed through thirteen brides. People are getting extremely suspicious. It's a wonder I'm getting another offer of marriage at all. As it is, this princess Ziqqora might be my very last chance to achieve wedded bliss. If you mess this up, I'll be stuck as a bachelor forever. *We'll* be stuck as a bachelor forever. The throne of Pecoz will be barren, bequeathed to some idiotic cousin. We'll be miserable, celibate, alone…"

Think outside the box, man. We don't have to be married to get our kicks!

"But I *want* to be married. I have to be, for the sake of the kingdom. Can't you let one of them live?"

The serpent gave a sigh, as if indulging a child.

Okay, he said. *I'll spare this one, I promise. Just as long as you make sure we get plenty of action on the side. And no more codpiece after the wedding, okay?*

"It's a deal," said Heinrich.

Having seemingly arrived at an accord with the creature, Heinrich bathed in silence in the stream. Still, he felt a little insecure. The serpent had made many promises before, and broken every one. He had to be sure that he could trust it this time. But how?

Suddenly he came upon a plan. He rushed to the bank, dried off and dressed himself, trapping the beast in the codpiece, then set off towards the nearest town.

When they arrived there, they stopped in the square, outside a bordello. He could feel the creature slumbering. *Good,* he thought. Then he summoned his secretary and whispered instructions.

Soon, the arrangements were made, and Heinrich was standing in one of the brothel's many rooms. A blindfolded woman knelt on the bed, her peach-like behind hoisted high in the air. She was beautiful and lithe, the best to be had here; she could pass as a princess. The room was well-appointed, with silken curtains and a four-poster bed; it could pass as a royal wedding chamber.

"They say you're a prince," the woman murmured. 'That's why I have to wear this blindfold, so I can't see your face. That way, I won't be able to track you down and start asking for money if I bring forth a bastard. But how do I know that this isn't some trick? For all I know you're a leper. One minute you're humping away, then next I feel your dick fall off inside of me!"

"You needn't worry about that," said Heinrich. "Besides, could a leper afford this?"

He tossed a handful of coins on the bed. The woman felt them blindly, then grinned.

"Okay," she said, wriggling her backside. "Let's go. Bring out that royal sceptre!"

Heinrich unbelted his trousers and lowered the codpiece. The serpent dropped out limply, then drowsily rose up, glancing around. It took in the sight of the candlelight, the curtains, but most of all the woman's wriggling rump.

Huh? it asked. *Are we married already?*

Heinrich nodded. "Just remember your promise."

The serpent nodded back and stretched out towards the bed. It shook itself a little on the way, throwing off the shackles of sleep. Then it caught the woman's scent and whipped out towards her pussy like a viper, slithering inside with a single, deft motion.

Heinrich trembled as he shared the sensation. The serpent's

head was bathing in wetness and warmth. It started surging, slithering, pumping away.

She's pretty loose for a princess, he heard it say in his head. *Still, that just gives me more room to manoeuvre!*

It started surging deeper, faster. Its jade coils thickened. The woman bucked and moaned, as though she were getting the fuck of her life. Was it a display, Heinrich wondered, or was she truly shocked by the serpent's speed and girth? Either way he found it hard to consider such things in his present state of mind. The pleasure was growing, mounting towards a meridian. He stood a few feet from the bed, eyes closed, shuddering as the creature went to work, faster and faster, bringing them both towards a climax. It tapped the woman's cervix, tap, tap, tap –

Then spread its jaws wide and bit deep at the moment of orgasm.

"No!" shouted Heinrich.

He gripped the raging serpent at the base and tried to drag it back out of the woman, but he was too weak with pleasure to fight it. The woman screamed, crawling away on the bed, blood gushing out between her lips and the serpent's thrusting coils.

But the creature wouldn't let her escape. It plunged through the ruins of her cervix, spitting loops of semen as it went, then sank its cruel fangs into the uterus, squishing the springy material between them. Venom shot through its fangs, triggering another, even more powerful orgasm. Heinrich shuddered uncontrollably. Paralysed by venom the woman slumped forwards, her eyes open wide beneath the blindfold as the serpent ate her ovaries.

She died of shock a few moments later, and the serpent slid

out of her, grinning and covered with blood. Still weak from the aftermath, Heinrich beheld it with a quivering glare.

"You bastard!" he growled. "You promised!"

I know I did, said the creature, licking its fangs. *And I meant it, too, at the time. But that meat is just so tempting! Besides, you weren't exactly straight with me, either. That woman's not a princess – she's a whore!*

"How'd you know?"

I heard you both whispering, just before I woke up. And there were other clues, as well, like the taste of all those men she hadn't quite douched away. Why did you lie to me, Heinrich?

"I wanted to test you. I had to be sure that you'd keep to your word on the wedding night."

Looks like you'll just have to wait and see, huh, buddy?

The serpent laughed. Heinrich grit his teeth.

Don't be like that. You know you liked it too.

The creature was right. He *had* liked it – how could he not ? The serpent's awful pleasures were also his own. He'd felt its delight at every single interval – the two-fold climax of jism and venom exploding, the visceral pleasure of feeding on the soft, springy meat. But he couldn't admit the truth; he couldn't give the serpent that satisfaction. He glared at it, loathingly. If he'd looked in the mirror at that moment, he probably would've stared at his own face with that self-same expression. But the serpent just slithered and flickered its tongue, its eyes filled with post-orgasmic ecstasy.

* * *

Meanwhile, Ziqqora and Mycoz hovered high above the bed, observing the sinister scene with horror and disgust. The demon-spawn's casual aura had gone.

"This is definitely bad," he said.

"No shit," said Ziqqora, shuddering as she stared at the corpse on the bed.

The wedding was set to take place tomorrow. If she didn't figure out something, and fast, then that dead girl on the bed could be her.

***

"Sounds like the kingdom's really gone to the dogs," said Ziqqora's great-great-great grandfather, the last of the Mushroom Kings, whose name had been Boletus, and to which he still answered, despite being a transcendental mushroom-man.

Ziqqora had just finished telling him all about recent events, as well as the history of Myconia for the past few hundred years. She'd taken a deep breath, and started from the very beginning, narrating the closure of the garden, the kingdom's long slide into decline, her own mother's death during childbirth, followed by her father's foolish marriage to a woman with red-headed twins, at which point she finally proceeded to more present and horrible dangers, namely her forthcoming marriage to Heinrich Van Gruel, a man with a monster in his codpiece.

She sat with Boletus and Mycoz at a table that had seemingly been summoned from nowhere. King Boletus's court was there too, including all of the courtiers who'd turned into mushrooms, such as King Boletus' secretary, his chamberlain, his knights, even his cook. There were well over a dozen. One of them looked injured, his body riddled with wounds that shed light from inside, as though his skin were the shade of a vandalised lantern. Ziqqora asked him how he was. He merely said that he was fine, and that he'd just had a run-in with some hooligans, but the situation was completely in hand now. Then he smiled enigmatically.

Mycoz's brethren were there too. They'd descended from the portals in a host of strange shapes – figures of fire, glass, and gas – then quickly transformed into the likeness of handsome men and women. One of them, Fallon, bore the look of a child once again.

"We should slit all their gizzards!" he cried.

"That's not much of a plan," said Mycoz.

"Maybe not," said Ziqqora. "But I think I've got one!"

It was true. The act of narrating events had given her a handle on the whole situation. She felt like she might just have the means to save herself from destruction. But would it really work in real life? She'd always been a dreamer. She wasn't used to coming up with practical things! Then again, this was the realm of the spirit, the Demon's Dream. Perhaps she was now in her element?

She whispered the details of her plan to the others, and together they started to plot.

CHAPTER 9: WEDDING BELLS

"This is most irregular," said the queen as she sat down.

The long banquet table was outside, set up on the manicured lawn between the palace and the gardens. All of the wedding guests were being seated around it, King Riksmund's clan at one end, as was tradition, with Heinrich Van Gruel and his jade-coloured host at the opposite extremity. But the wedding hadn't actually *happened* yet, and the feast was not supposed to take place until *after* the ceremony.

"It was Ziqqora's request," said Riksmund. "And she was very adamant about it. She said she couldn't possibly go through the ceremony on an empty stomach, that she needed some food to smother all those butterflies flitting about in her stomach."

"You indulge her too much," said the queen. 'But then again, I suppose it *is* her wedding day."

She permitted herself a smile. Let the brat have this final indulgence, she thought. After tonight it wouldn't matter anyway – not after she'd shared a wedding bed with Heinrich Van Gruel.

At that, the queen found herself laughing. Her plan was so close to fruition she could taste it!

"What's so funny, my dear?" asked the king.

"Oh, nothing really. I suppose I'm just so happy for her!"

✢✢✢

Ziqqora's golden locks blazed in the sun, which sat at its apex above. She wore the traditional crimson gown made for virgin brides, symbolizing the blood that would soon be spilled out from her stretched-open hymen.

Not if I can help it! she thought.

She tried to smother her nervousness as she waited for the feast to begin. All she was doing was sitting at a table, and yet her blood was already pounding in her veins, as though she were running from a wolf. In a way, she was. She took a glance at Van Gruel, who was seated a few dozen feet away from her, surrounded by his courtiers and knights. He too wore red in anticipation of the marriage bed. But the bastard was stained with blood already, she thought.

She avoided his gaze as he glanced back towards her. The queen let out a sigh.

"Just look how shy she is! She'll soon get over that. Just like I did, the first time I was married."

"You certainly weren't shy with me," said the king.

They giggled and canoodled beside one another. Ziqqora managed a forced smile, but it was more like a grimace. She glanced at her stepsisters. Usually the little brats would be full of piss and vinegar, especially at a time like this. Usually they'd be poking out their tongues and exalting in her misery. But today they looked sick and lethargic. Their faces were pastier than ever, and some of their freckles had begun to turn black. Ziqqora smiled to herself, darkly, and waited for the feast.

Soon it came, a barrage of food in twelve courses. First soup, then pheasant, then venison, then pie, then a whole bunch of other dishes to which Ziqqora didn't really pay attention. There was only one thing she was focused on – the familiar, bitter flavour that tainted each and every dish, from the gravy to the plum sauce to the wine in her glass.

At length the feast was over and everyone was full as they could be. She saw the wedding guests stirring uncomfortably, longing to unbuckle their belts and give their bloated bellies some breathing room, but they still had the ceremony to get through.

Together they left the table and headed to the podium on the grass nearby. There stood the master of ceremonies, wearing his mystical robes. The guests took up position before him, arranging themselves into two long rows with an aisle in between, down which Van Gruel strode first, cheered on by his comrades and kinfolk. Then came Ziqqora, accompanied by her father. The feeling of his hand around hers made her nauseous with anger. How could he have let this all happen?

Soon he'll discover the error of his ways, she thought.

He left her by Van Gruel's side in front of the altar. Was that a tear in his eye? And if so, was it from happiness, pride, or bitter regret?

She didn't have time to imagine. Van Gruel was before her, a tower of muscle and might. His handsome face smiled, but his codpiece stood between them, pregnant with death. Was that a flicker of movement from within? She cast down her eyes, and played the demure, blushing bride.

Then the master of ceremonies began.

"Ladies and gentlemen, we are gathered here today to join this couple in wedlock. I'd like to call upon the demons to witness this union from their castles in the void. May they devour those who seek to defile or betray it. May they rend them with claws and ravage their orifices aplenty."

The rite master paused, muttering strange words intended to draw down the eyes of the demons. Then he continued.

"And now for the oaths," he said. "Heinrich Van Gruel, do you take this woman to be your wedded wife, to thrill her with your body whenever she desires, to bring harm to her enemies and joy to her friends, to bring fire to her hearth and warmth to her bed, to keep the rats from her legs and the lice from her hair, to defend her from brigands and zombies and trolls, to keep her furnace well-stoked and her flowerbed moist, to pay heed to her words and accept her caresses, to brandish your torch and bring light to her nights, to never lose sight of the tiller-man sitting in her boat, to get behind the oxen and plough her wet grass, to yank on the rope that rings bells in her belfry, to fill her warm slipper right up to the toe, until the terms of your union be dissolved?"

"I do," said Van Gruel.

"And do you, Ziqqora of Myconia, take this man to be your wedded husband, to…"

Ziqqora felt her blood begin to pound even faster as the master of ceremonies droned out the vow. Something was wrong; her plan should've gone into effect by now. This whole thing should be over! Instead she stood there as if in a trance, only half-hearing the words. She felt somehow distant, alien to herself, just as she'd felt when she'd travelled in the spirit and seen her own sleeping body in the grove down below. This couldn't be her, here, now, by the podium – she couldn't be forced to this hideous oath!

She grew faint. Nausea bubbled in her stomach. But was it from fear, or a sign of her deliverance? The air began to bubble and ripple in front of her. She felt light and airy, as if she were about to pass out. Perhaps she'd swoon, and he'd carry her off to the marriage bed anyway? It'd been known to happen. She'd wake with the serpent inside of her, eating her organs.

She fought to stay standing. Then the air became filled with a kaleidoscope of colours that swayed like a curtain in front of her.

At last! she thought, then drew aside the curtain, and stepped across the breach.

CHAPTER 10: CHANGE OF VENUE

Ziqqora smiled. She stood in the Demon's vibrant Dream. The rest of the wedding guests were there too, muttering or shouting or screaming in terror.

"What the fuck's going on?" said one.

"Oh shit!" said a second.

"AAAHHHH!" said a third.

In the distance arose the monolithic structure that was home to the statue of the demon's nameless mother. Closer by stood Mycoz and his brethren, as well as King Boletus and his transcendental court, gathered round the wedding guests in luminous, humanoid shapes.

Steadily the guests began to calm themselves, if only a little.

"What's the meaning of this?" shouted King Riksmund. "Where are we?"

"In the Demon's Dream," said Ziqqora. "I dosed all the food in the kitchen with mushrooms, right before the feast. That's why I wanted to eat before the ceremony. So I could bring us all here, and show you the truth."

Her voice was steady now, so too her pose. She felt safer, more powerful here. But she knew that the struggle was very far from over.

"Foolish girl!" snapped her father. "I told you the mushrooms were poisonous. This is all a trap! They're going to eat us, turn us into fungus, just like poor Boletus —"

"Shut up, Dad!" she snapped. "You don't know what you're talking about. The demons are our allies. And Boletus's right there!"

She pointed to the last of the Mushroom Kings, who waved to his great-great grandson and smiled.

"Hello young man," he said, even though King Riksmund was hoary with age. "You should listen to your daughter, you know. She's a very clever girl."

Riksmund just stood there, speechless.

"This place isn't a trap," said Ziqqora. "The wedding was a trap – for me! That bitch wife of yours is trying to kill me. Van Gruel isn't a man, he's an abomination. Just look at what he's got in his codpiece!"

She ripped off her bridegroom's groin guard, then leapt back at once as the serpent whipped out of it, snarling. Cries of shock erupted from the crowd. Van Gruel himself stood as if stunned, making no move to cover or hide what had been revealed.

"See?" she said. "He's not just well-hung – he's a monster down there!"

The king stared in horror at Van Gruel's flailing member. Then he turned to his wife.

"You knew about this?" he asked.

"Of course not!" she snapped. "Besides, this is all a lie, a delusion, a trick – we've all been drugged!"

"You're the liar," said Ziqqora. "But soon you won't lie anymore."

She grinned darkly as blood stared dripping from her stepmother's eyes.

"What's…what's going on?!" the queen cried. Ziqqora knew

she'd be feeling the pain in her physical body too, even though here she wore the form of a spirit.

The queen's bleeding eyes glanced around for her daughters, but they were not to be found in this dreamscape. Ziqqora's grin widened, seeing events unfold on both sides of the curtain. The red-headed brats, being effectively already dead, no longer had souls with which to enter the dreaming. Their bodies had been hollowed from within and infested by the spores of black fungus, which filled them with its own savage purpose.

Out there in that physical world, they dragged their mother's unconscious body on top of the banquet table and worked out her eyes with a pair of silver forks. The mutilation was mirrored in the dreamscape, her stepmother's bloodied eyeballs popping out of their sockets to dangle on glistening nerves. The sight of it reminded her of a cup-and-ball toy she used to play with as a child. But while Ziqqora might've been able to whip up that ball into its rightful position, her stepmother's eyeballs would never go back in, neither in this world, nor in the other.

Then the woman's flesh started blistering and bubbling, her daughters having tossed her into a boiling cauldron of soup. The king screamed in horror as he saw what was happening. He reached out to his wife, but her skin just sloughed off in his hands, like slivers of pork in a broth.

Ziqqora turned back to the still-stunned Van Gruel.

"As for you," she said, "this wedding is cancelled!"

Van Gruel just stood there a moment longer, paralysed, his gaze far away as if fighting a battle in his head with the thing between his legs. They shared one body, after all. Maybe, in the physical world, Van Gruel had been in charge of that body – most of it, anyway. But the serpent was a creature from Beyond, and had more power in the dreaming than he did. It must have roiled into his mind like smoke into a chimney, forcing him back into the corners of his psyche and taking him over completely, because when Van Gruel finally spoke, it was not with his own voice, but with the sibilant cadence of a serpent.

"I don't think so, bitch," he said. "This is a wedding, and I didn't just come to eat cake. Men – kill these clowns!"

Van Gruel's knights drew their blades and rushed towards Mycoz and his kindred. The demon-spawn responded by assuming their terrifying battle-shapes. Ziqqora saw Fallon rise up into the form of a crocodile with iridescent scales and fungal protrusions. He seized a knight in his jaws and bit the doomed man in half. Blood exploded out from the man's dying spirit like streaks of red lightning.

Suddenly Mycoz was ten feet tall and wading into battle right beside his little brother. His eyes were bright red and his skin was dark purple. He ripped a man's head off with claws like an eagle's.

Then the Mushroom King's forces charged deep into the fray, riding on steeds made of pure hallucination, striking down their enemies with psychedelic blades. The dreamscape was a riot of screaming and blood.

But Ziqqora didn't have time to pay much attention to the battle, for Van Gruel was heading towards her, staring with two sets of eyes. The expression in each was the same, a glower of murderous lust.

CHAPTER II: DEVOURED

Ziqqora darted backwards and concentrated, transforming her dress into a suit of steel armour. It encased her whole body, except for the head. Her golden hair cascaded down her back like a cape. A sword appeared in her right hand, raised for the kill.

Now it was Van Gruel's turn to leap backwards as she slashed at his serpentine phallus. He dodged the blow expertly, then glared at her, while the battle kept raging all around them, blood and gore exploding in the dreaming like a fireworks display.

"Nice trick," he hissed with his sibilant voice. "But two can play at that game."

The serpent flexed its otherworldly will. Suddenly Van Gruel was likewise covered in sleek, shining armour, which extended all the way to the head of his murderous phallus. The serpent writhed and wriggled, flexing the moulded steel scales that now covered its coils. At the same time a blade appeared in Van Gruel's right hand, with which he slashed at Ziqqora.

She fended off the blow, no stranger to swordplay by now, having been tutored by some of Mycoz's allies. She'd been under the instruction of the blood-drinking duellists of Zimoa for what felt like weeks, but barely minutes had passed in Myconia's physical realm. She struck back at Van Gruel with a brutal swipe, catching the side of the serpent with her blade. It whipped away, growling, bruised but protected by its armour.

"Not bad," said Van Gruel. "But none of this will save you. You can bolster your hymen with steel, but I'm still gonna break it. You can stab me with your sword, but it's you who'll get skewered in the end. Still, I have to commend you. It's good to have some foreplay for a change!"

He rushed her, swinging his blade as the serpent whipped out from his crotch. Ziqqora struggled to defend against the two deadly weapons at once. She knocked back his blade time and again, only for the snake to come hissing at her face, or striking down low at her groin, trying to rip off her armour or bite its way through to her flesh. No sooner would she beat aside the beast than his sword would come swinging again, straining her defences to their limit. The strength behind his blows was incredible. Was it powered by Van Gruel's mutant might, or the will of the serpent? It was difficult to tell in the dreaming, where the force of mind and muscle overlapped and conjoined.

She wielded her blade desperately, fending off the blows, sweating, getting tired. As good as her training had been, she just wasn't ready to duel with Van Gruel. She had to escape!

After striking wildly, making some space for herself to manoeuvre, she leapt up and flew towards a portal above.

* * *

"Get back here!" shouted Van Gruel with the voice of the serpent. "I've got a down-payment on that pussy!"

He pursued her through the portal, emerging into a starscape. Of course, such sights were not strange to the mind of the serpent, who'd been called from the realms beyond earth.

He saw his delectable quarry on a road made of meteoric dust. Her armour gleamed in the light of distant stars. Her hair framed her hips like a nimbus of gold. The serpent felt his coils getting thicker, bulging with an influx of blood. The pressure was almost enough to bend his armour out of shape. He had to have her, now!

He flew on towards her, and landed nearby. In the distance was a cloud of debris, made up of space junk and glittering fragments of god's blood, all of it frozen by the cold of the void. Something massive had lain there once, something the size of a planetoid, but now it was gone, devoured or destroyed, leaving nought but a big cloud of rubble in its wake.

But the serpent didn't care about that. He wasn't here to map out the space-ways. He was here for one thing, and one thing only!

He rushed at Ziqqora, commanding Van Gruel's body like a puppet's. Dimly he could hear the protestations of his host, coming from the corners of their commingled psyche. He didn't care about those, either. Van Gruel's body was his now, just as it always should've been.

He swung at the princess, then struck with his fangs. She fended off the blows, but only barely. She was weakening, crumbling, succumbing to his might. It wouldn't be long until he had her in his coils!

He lashed out again, striking the sword from her hand. She looked back with wide, frightened eyes, like a doe about to flee before the hounds of the hunt. The expression on her face only deepened his arousal. He cast aside his sword and gripped her breastplate with his fingers, while his serpentine head shot up towards her crotch, tearing at the chainmail that lay beneath the tassets. He could smell her sweet scent through the ringlets of steel. Soon he'd be bathing in it, swimming in it. He wrenched with all his might, ripping off the breastplate and the armour below.

A shower of gore shot from the breach and splattered him all over, reeking of days-old death.

Oh crap, he thought. *Did I kill her? Already?*

He felt a wave of immediate disappointment. Ravaging her corpse wouldn't be nearly as fun as impaling her soft, living body. He blinked the rancid blood away, and his own eyes went wide.

The armour he'd peeled from that beautiful body had been nought but the cover of a gore-stuffed cushion. The girl's golden hair, nothing but a wig. The serpent had been duped!

He looked around, spotting the princess floating high in the void. She was naked and smiling, dancing lasciviously. Her nubile fingers plucked at her nipples and played in her pubes. Her slender legs flexed and cavorted, framed by a mane of golden hair.

"You fucking tease!" he roared.

* * *

Ziqqora kept grinning, but it was almost a rictus. She danced in the most wanton manner possible, even as her mind recoiled from the act of dancing for Van Gruel. Still, she had to keep his attention focused tightly on her body. Her whole plan depended on this gamble.

All the pieces were in place but one. She'd conjured the dummy into existence with the magick that Mycoz's allies had taught her. She'd even abandoned her armour and weapon to make his false victory seem even more convincing; she barely had the strength left to summon more arms if they were needed. Thus, she was well and truly tied to her present course of action. If it failed, she was screwed – literally, and to death! But would the final ingredient fall into place?

Her question was answered as the stars behind Van Gruel began to vanish. Suddenly she didn't know what to fear most – Van Gruel, or the thing that had arrived, seeking the reeking gore that he wore, swimming just under the skin of the void, visible only by the shifting lacuna of starlight covering its gigantic body like camouflage.

Van Gruel flew towards her, away from the patch of seething darkness. Not because he'd seen the threat, of course – he only had eyes for her, two sets of eyes frenzied with lust.

Fuck, thought Ziqqora. *He's moving out of position!*

She took a deep breath and flew towards the darkness, overshooting Van Gruel from above. He growled, turned, and gave chase, his four eyes chained to her gleaming white body.

Ziqqora sensed the terrible presence before her, could almost smell its stench, that of all the world's abattoirs at once. She drew as close as she dared, then veered off in another direction. Van Gruel followed, gaining ground. Her movements, seemingly random and flitting, had allowed him to close very quickly.

He reached for her. She felt his armoured fingers scraping her skin, grasping only emptiness, just as something drew wide beneath *him*. A set of great jaws emerged from the darkness, colossal and hungry and stinking, with teeth like white reefs in a bubbling blood ocean, strewn with the skins of dead gods slowly rotting.

Krauwm, the Demon Worm, was here!

And just as ugly as the first time Ziqqora had seen him, back during her very first trip. The smell of the gore covering Van

Gruel had lured the beast from his feeding grounds, exactly as she'd hoped it would.

Van Gruel's eyes flashed with terror and anger. He let out a roar of inchoate rage and reached for Ziqqora again, catching at her ankle. She shook herself free as the jaws of the demon engulfed him. Van Gruel's head and hands jutted between the Worm's shuttered teeth like the limbs of a criminal condemned to the stocks. He looked at her, no longer with the lust of the serpent, but with the gaze of a man filled with something like relief. Then the worm ground its teeth, slicing both man and serpent to pieces, and his face was no more.

Ziqqora sped back through the portal and into the Demon's bright realm. Van Gruel's knights had all been slaughtered, their bodies torn asunder. Her father wept on his knees, cradling the body of his wife, who'd now been reduced to little more than a puddle of flesh around steaming bones. His own soldiers had surrendered to Mycoz and the demon-spawn, some of whom were injured, their bodies leaking blood that shone like bright lightning and travelled like squid ink underwater. Her ancestor Boletus stood alongside them, as did his courtiers, wearing their psychedelic robes.

Ziqqora landed before her father, then remembered, she was naked!

She summoned a set of bright robes that mirrored the dress of the Mushroom King. Atop her head, she created a crown, with tines like mushroom stalks and a dome of bright fabric resembling the cap of a toadstool.

"Dad," she said, "we need to talk."

CHAPTER 12: THE COURT OF THE MUSHROOM QUEEN

Ziqqora the First ascended to the throne following her father's abrupt abdication.

The first thing she did was change the royal livery back to the symbol of a toadstool with a crown on the top. The second thing she did was have the iron fence around the garden removed and replaced with a fortified wall. The place remained forbidden to all but herself and a few chosen courtiers. Uninvited visitors would be captured and slaughtered by the regiment of soldiers who guarded the stock of royal mushrooms by night and by day.

For the mushrooms were said to grant fabulous visions, and the queen consumed them often, gaining the knowledge she needed to govern Myconia with wisdom and might.

Or so people say. Others just think that she liked to get high.

Perhaps the proof is in the pudding, for the queen showed an uncanny knack for diplomacy and trade. Pretty soon, her kingdom grew prosperous once more. The palace was rebuilt from its crumbling foundations. The neighbouring kingdom of Pecoz was conquered, its rulers sent into exile. Their sorcerers, the Sebeks, were rounded up and burned at the stake. Otherwise the people were spared and made subjects of Myconia.

The queen did take a husband, but kept him consigned to

the status of a prince, denying him a share in her rule. She married him for one reason only: to help produce heirs for the throne of Myconia, a task at which he duly succeeded, giving her five noble children, two girls and three boys.

But it was said that his life, though luxurious and filled with undeniable nookie, was something of a sad one. The poor prince was a notorious cuckold. Everyone knew that the queen had a lover with the body of a toadstool and the soul of a demon. She visited him often, whenever she ate of the mushrooms that grew in the garden.

In time, she grew old, as all mortals must do. Her flesh became withered and her hair became white. She left the kingdom to her heirs and went off into the garden, where her body transformed. Her skin became fibrous and sprouting, her sweat became motes of white spores, and her toes spread like roots into the soil.

But her soul went off to journey through the Demon's bright Dreaming, where she dwells as she did in her youth, with long golden locks and a soft nubile figure. She's probably there to this day, wrapped in the arms of her lover as they fuck beneath moonbeams or dance around planets to the tune of a song with no ending.

About the Author

B.J. Swann writes punk AF fiction with elements of fantasy, extreme horror, erotica, and anything else he wants to throw in there. The Aeon of Chaos is his fictional setting, a hyper-reality of fairytale madness where anything can happen.

Website: www.aeonofchaos.com

Contact: bjswann@aeonofchaos.com

By B.J. Swann and Elizabeth Bedlam

Holocaust Hearts

Two hearts bound across fathomless distance, haloed in fire that will murder the world.

A lot of devils are proud of Hell, but Silfer isn't one of them. He's bored with the torture and endless visceral depravity. He's bored with infernal politics. He's even bored with the charms of the lascivious succubus sisters – and that's really saying something. He's bored, he's bored, he's bored - and his secret, lonely heart is home to a fathomless longing.

Up on Earth, Mara is drowning in muted grey misery. She hates her job restoring antique books at the local museum. She hates the house-flipping yuppies who've infested her neighbourhood and made it so disgustingly trendy. She hates her busybody boss Kathy, who seems committed to making her life a misery with unwanted friendship. With a longing both nameless and consuming she dreams of something far beyond her daily banality.

One day she recieves a box of mouldering books from the bowels of a faraway church. Nestled like refuse amongst the tomes are a series of loose pages made from calfskin – or something very like it. They speak to her in whispers and hell-fire dreams. Unbenowkst to Mara, she's stumbled on the lost pages of the *Codex Infernalis Futuatis*, the most terrible book ever to be released from the gates of Hell. As Silfer seeks the book, his world collides with Mara's, and their hearts become bound in a love that will forever devour them both – and have terrible consequences of the rest of the universe.

From the combined pens of Elizabeth Bedlam, queen of offbeat erotic horror, and B.J. Swann, creator of the Aeon of Chaos, Holocaust Hearts is a black romantic comedy steeped in carnage, depravity, and total hilarity. You've never read anything like it.

Also by B.J. Swann

Our Lady of the Scythe

"Hogwarts and Camp Halfblood, move the HELL over; there's a new boarding school in town and it is **not** for the kiddies!" - Christine Morgan, Splatterpunk Award-winning author of Lakehouse Infernal

Eighteen-year-old Raza has a problem. Every time she tries to get busy with a boy, she turns into a monster and tears him apart. Why? Because her father is the Big Horned Bastard, demon supreme. To unlock the mysteries of her birthright - and hopefully get some sex education - she's sent to Our Lady of the Scythe, a boarding school for demon-spawn where detention is a realm of flesh-eating monsters and the delinquents get their kicks out of mass murder. Will she even survive the first semester? And what happens when she and her new friends stumble on a vile angelic plot that threatens the survival of all demonkind? Raza will have to embrace her inner demon fast, or kiss her butt goodbye.

Our Lady of the Scythe: Demon Academy is a Punk As Fuck riff on the supernatural boarding school genre. It contains graphic sex, violence, and potentially disturbing material. It is not intended for children or the easily offended.

Also by B.J. Swann

The Crimson Crown

Inverted Dreams. Excoriated Hearts. Terror and Horror Sublime.

The twin princesses Oda and Honey are as different as night and day. Oda is a child of the dark, obsessed with cruelty and death. Honey is as sweet as her name, filled with goodwill and compassion. It is therefore a remarkably revolting twist of fate when the royal astrologer orders Oda to be married to the mild-mannered King Armand, while Honey is betrothed to King Barbus of Gutgirt, the most brutal man in the world, who tears peasants apart with his bare hands and keeps his murdered brides' bodies on display in his own bloody chamber.

As the twins strive to wrest back their lives from the cruel hand of fate, they embark on a journey of self discovery that will twist them in unimaginable ways – and perhaps bare the secrets of their innermost selves. At the centre of their struggles, shining balefully over all, is the Crimson Crown of Gutgirt, a relic of terrible mystery and demonic power, whose secrets hold the key to salvation – and everlasting doom.

The Crimson Crown is a Punk as Fuck fantasy story set in the Aeon of Chaos. It contains graphic sex, violence, and potentially disturbing material. It is not intended for children or the easily offended.

Also by B.J. Swann

The Second Wolf

Bestial Violence. Monstrous Lust. Total Mayhem.

A Beast stalks the forests and moors around the city of Stubbe, raping and killing by night, vanishing by day. As the bodies of mangled victims pile up, the citizens grow increasingly terrified – and violent. Unable to stop or trap the elusive Beast, or fathom the cause of its inhuman lusts, the local constabulary is forced to seek help from an outsider in the form of Rubria Caracalla, a beautiful monster hunter of vague but lethal reputation. But Rubria is no ordinary monster hunter, and her perverted plans for the Beast are not the same as those of her patrons.

"The Second Wolf" is a Punk as Fuck fantasy story set in the Aeon of Chaos. It contains graphic sex, violence, and potentially disturbing material. It is not intended for children or the easily offended.

Available exclusively from www.godless.com

Also by B.J. Swann

The Unwithering Flower

Unbridled greed. Dark necromancy. Total Mayhem.

When Narseh the Slaver journeys to the infamous City of Whores, he thinks he's about to make a fortune trading in nubile human flesh. Instead he finds the city's population decimated by plague. His sordid mercantile venture looks utterly doomed – until a chance encounter with a beautiful sorceress changes everything. By combining her necromantic powers with his commercial know-how, the new allies use the site of the plague-ridden city to launch a money-making scheme so devious, so vile, so repulsive, that it will live on in infamy forever, and bring a storm of vengeance and bloodshed down upon their heads the likes of which the City of Whores has never seen.

The Unwithering Flower is a punk AF fantasy story featuring extreme horror and irreverent humour, set in the Aeon of Chaos. It contains graphic sex, violence, and potentially disturbing material. It is not intended for children or the easily offended.

Available in Print and Digital from Amazon